FIX-IT DUCK

For Clare

Fix-It Duck

Copyright © 2001 by Jez Alborough

Printed in the U.S.A. All rights reserved.

www.harperchildrens.com

Library of Congress Cataloging-in-Publication Data

Alborough, Jez.

   Fix-It Duck / Jez Alborough.

      p.   cm.

Summary: Duck's attempts to deal with various minor disasters only lead to more problems.

ISBN 0-06-000699-4

[1. Repairing—Fiction.   2. Ducks—Fiction.   3. Animals—Fiction.

4. Stories in rhyme.]   I. Title.

PZ8.3.A33 Fi   2002

[E]—dc21   2001024964

          8 9 10 ❖

First U.S. edition, HarperCollins Publishers, Inc., 2002

Originally published in Great Britain by

HarperCollins Publishers Ltd., 2001

Jez Alborough
FIX-IT DUCK

HarperCollins*Publishers*

Plop! goes the drip that drops in the cup.
Duck looks down and Duck looks up.

"A leak in the roof.
Oh, what bad luck!

This is a job for . . .

FIX-IT DUCK."

He says, "It's easy to repair."
But how's he going to reach up there?

He can't climb up—
it's much too steep.

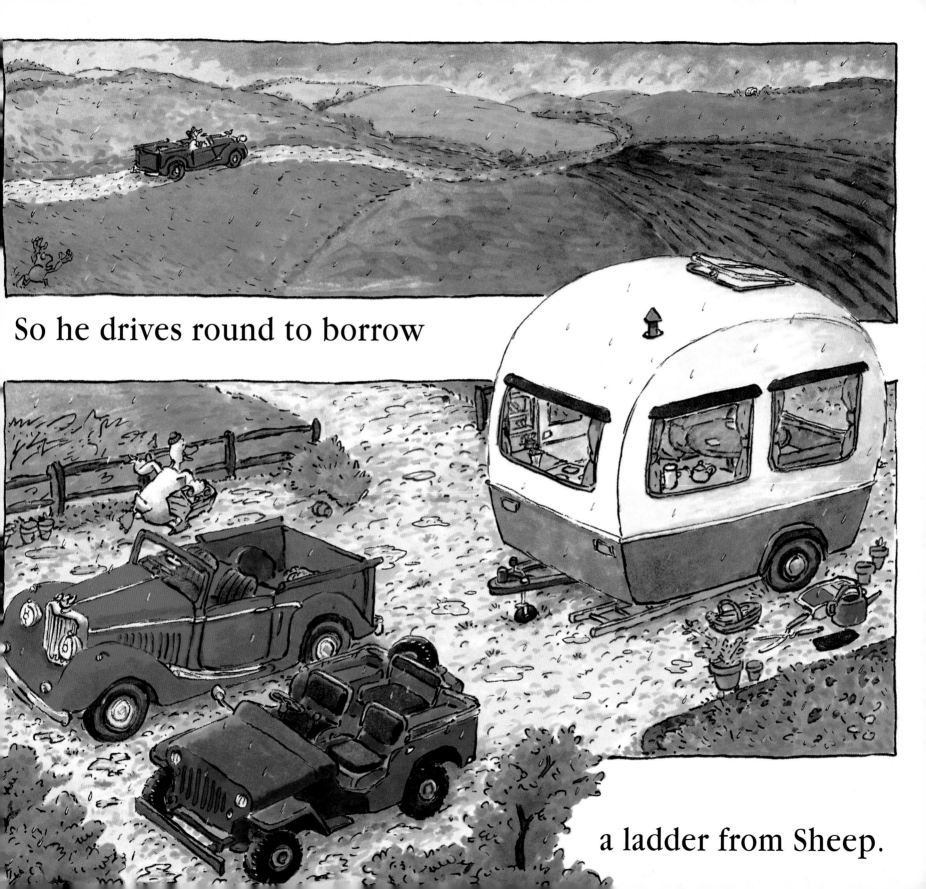

So he drives round to borrow

a ladder from Sheep.

Over the puddles
he hops and he skips,

to Sheep's little house,
then, *OOPS*, he trips!

"Sheep!" calls Duck.
"It's only me."

And he explains how the rain
had dripped in his tea.

When he reaches the part about fixing the leak,
they hear a rattle, creak, and squeak.

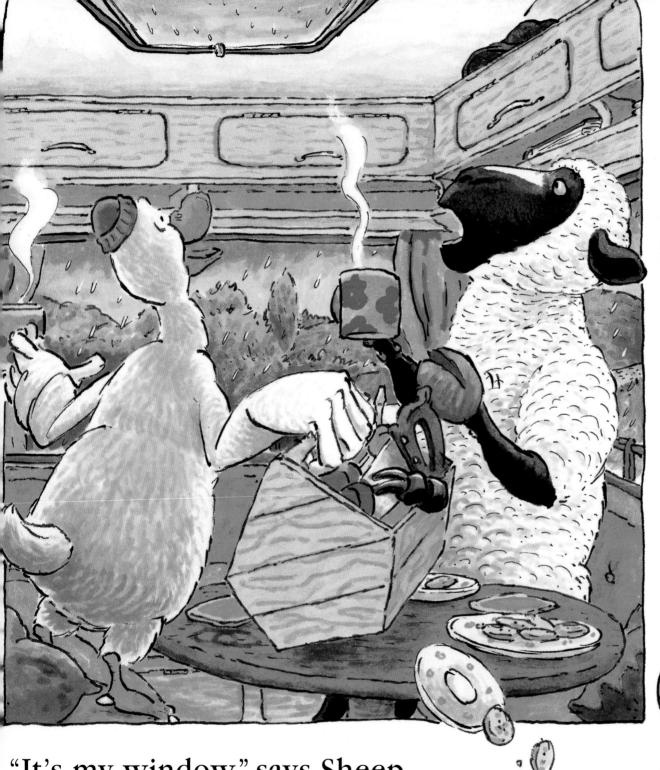

"It's my window," says Sheep.
"It won't close. It's stuck."

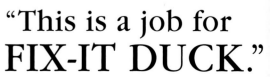

"This is a job for
FIX-IT DUCK."

He does what he can to close up the gap.
He glues it, screws it, and gives it a tap.

"The problem," says Duck, "is your glass is too thin."
"My house," wails Sheep. "The rain's coming in!"

"What we need," says Duck, with a glint in his eye,
"is to pull your house to somewhere dry.

Goat's got a shed. We can put it inside.
Let's hook up your Jeep and go for a ride.

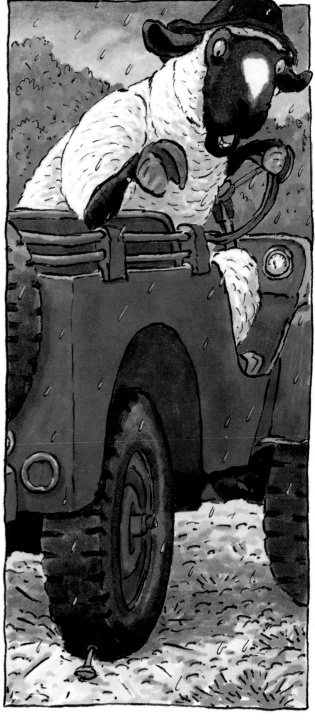

Back up slowly,
till I say stop."

Then all of a sudden,
something goes *POP!*

"Flat tire!" says Duck. "More bad luck.
We'll have to use my pickup truck."

But Sheep's little house won't hitch to the truck.

"This is a job for . . .   FIX-IT DUCK."

"We're off," says Duck as they speed down the track.

"Slow down on the bends," calls Sheep from the back.

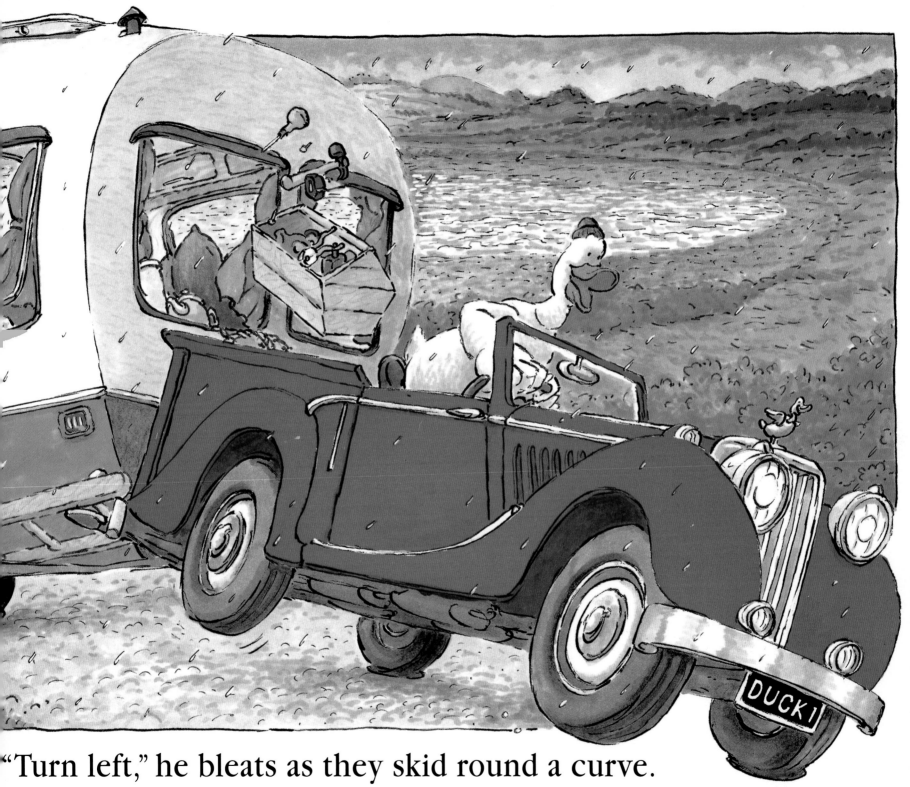

"Turn left," he bleats as they skid round a curve.
"Hold on tight," quacks Duck as the truck starts to swerve.

And the house should follow behind but instead . . .

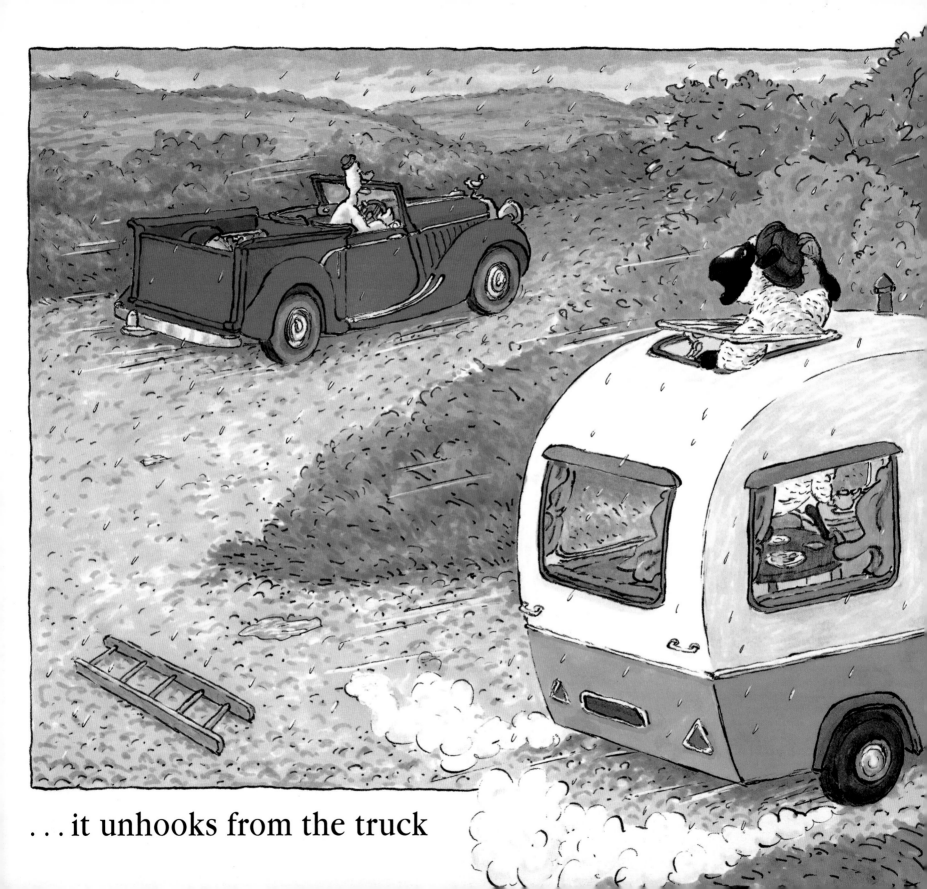

...it unhooks from the truck

and rolls on straight ahead.

When Duck gets to Goat's, he starts to explain
why they'd brought Sheep's house, which was letting in rain.

"But where is it?" asks Goat.
Then as Duck turns to see,

Frog runs up, shouting,
"It's following me!"

"Look up the hill,"
gasps Goat in dismay.

"It's Sheep," quacks Duck,
"and he's coming this way!"

"Run!" cries Frog.
"He's going to crash!"

"H - E - L - P!" bleats Sheep.

"It's broken," says Duck. "What a lot of bad luck."

"Oh, no!" moans Sheep, "*not ...* FIX-IT